# TIME FLIES

ERIC ROHMANN     Crown Publishers, Inc., *New York*

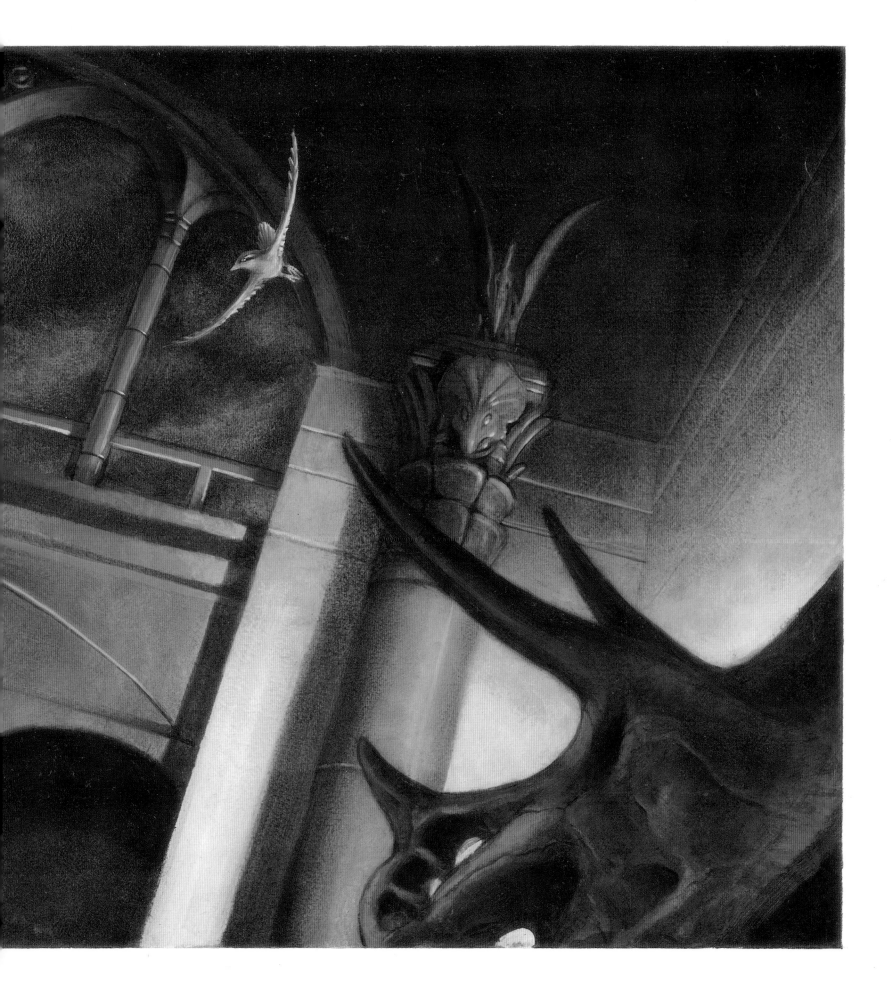

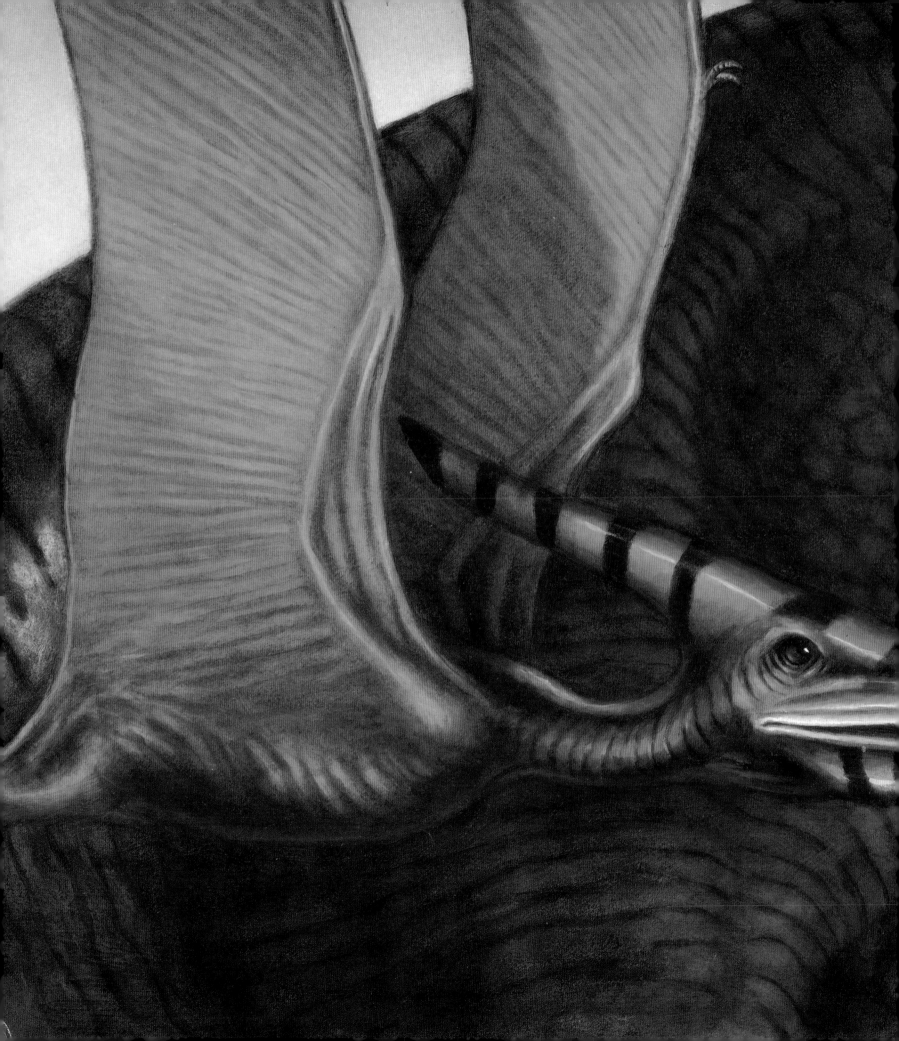

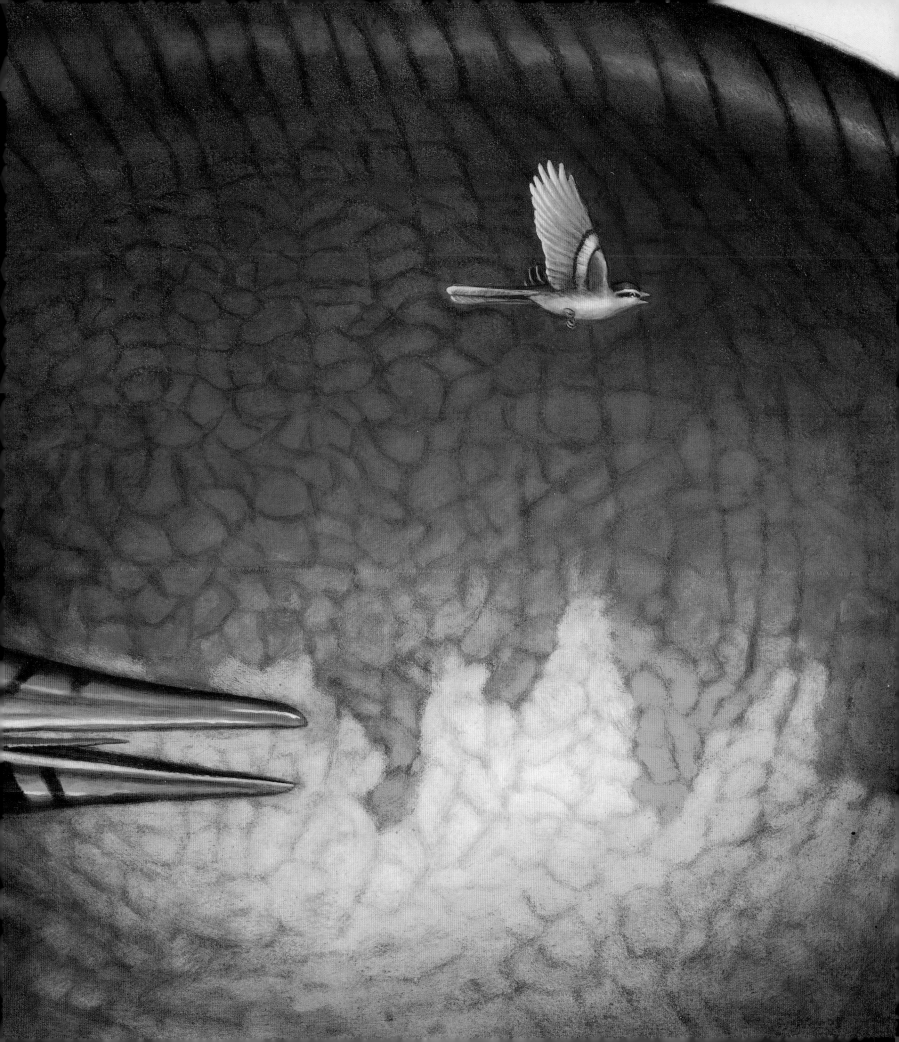

CROWN is a trademark of Crown Publishers, Inc.
Manufactured in the United States of America
*Library of Congress Cataloging-in-Publication Data*
Rohmann, Eric.
Time flies / by Eric Rohmann.
p.   cm.
Summary: A wordless tale in which a bird flying around the dinosaur exhibit in a natural history museum has an unsettling experience when
the dinosaur seems to come to life and view the bird as a potential meal.
[1. Stories without words. 2. Birds—Fiction. 3. Dinosaurs—Fiction. 4. Museums—Fiction.] I. Title.
PZ7.R6413Ti                              1994
[E]—dc20         93-28200
ISBN 0-517-59598-2 (trade)
0-517-59599-0 (lib. bdg.)
10  9  8  7  6  5  4  3